DEAR MS

JOAN POULSON

ILLUSTRATED BY
CHARLOTTE HARD

A & C BLACK • LONDON

For Chaz

Tuesday September 18th

Tuesday September 18

Dear Ms
write me a letter, you said.

So I'm writing,
but only because you said.
My dad thinks writing letters
to teachers is stupid.
I think letters are more for girls.

And I'm not being cheeky
but you said we could be honest
and I think if you've nothing better to do

than read letters from us lot
and write us letters back
there's a problem in this school.

   Dead Bored.
   So bored I've nearly stopped breathing.

                    David Helston

PS There is a problem.
It's called GIRLS.

Monday September 24th

Hiya Kate, d'you think Ms is going mad dribbling on like that about communication? What's wrong with mobiles, best thing since they invented football!!!! When you going to get one?
Love Mandy

Mandy, I can't. You don't know what my mum's like, worst thing since Cruella. Kate

Tuesday September 25th

Tuesday September 25

Dear Ms

yawn, yawn, yawn.
Oh sorry, didn't see you there.

Oh, now I'm sorrier still.
The bell's just gone
and I've not written my letter

I've got to go now.
Arrrggghhh - that's me
forcing myself to put my pen down.

In tears.
David Helston

Tuesday, September 25th

Dear Ms,

I liked the joke about hedgehogs –
too many points.
That's good (ish).

I still don't get it though.
What's writing letters got to do with school
or even with real life?

From Questioning Kate

8

How d'ya get my number, Tracey? Yeah, it's cool. I'm really really glad I've got one.

AW, THAT'D BE TELLING! TRACE THE ACE GETS PLACES OTHER KIDS DON'T KNOW!!! ANYWAY, WHAT DO YOU THINK ABOUT US BEING BEST FRIENDS? IT MAKES SENSE BECAUSE WE LIVE NEAR EACH OTHER AND WE BOTH DO FOOTBALL.

Yeah, but I do it because I love it, you do it because of the boyz!!!!

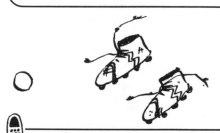

BUT IT STILL MAKES SENSE. AND WHAT ABOUT YOU WITH STEVE?

Aw Tracey, shuddup will you and get off my back.

Friday September 28th

REMINDER

Anyone from Year 6 who might be interested in the School Football Club meet in the Hall on Tuesday (2nd October) at 3.45.

You must bring a signed letter of permission from home.

J Harding

Kate, what d'you think? Will you come to Football Club? I promise you I'm going to get on the team!!! Mandy

Dear Mandy, you on the team? They'd be better off having Posh Spice, luv Kate

I don't think so!!! Anyway, she doesn't go to Waterside Primary, does she!! love Mandy

No, a shame, that. She might've brought Becks!!! We've just got fat Tracey luv from Kate

Monday October 1st

Dear Kate, you never said if you'll come to Football Club tomorrow. Will you? love Mandy

It's a bit pointless asking. I know The Mad Cow'll not let me, luv Kate.

But promise you'll ask!!! lots of love
* Mandy

Monday October 1st

Dear Ms,

I can't write about things
I'm interested in
because there's nothing I'm interested
in that you'd be interested in too.

Like soccer.

That's all I'm interested in after school.
Well, or in school, too.
And computers,
I'm dead keen on computers.

And I'm not being cheeky,
I know girls have soccer teams

but it's not really soccer they play is it?
You should hear my dad about that.

   still yawning
      because what's the use
         when you think what
            we could be doing instead,
              this avvie

                David Helston

Kate, I think she's really really lost it!!!!! All this about letters! Did you know you can get mobiles dead cheap now? Mandy

Hi, Mandy, Sorry this is short. Ms is watching. I don't want to get caught. DON'T talk about mobiles being cheap. My mum is DEAD DEAD TIGHT luv Kate

Tuesday October 2nd

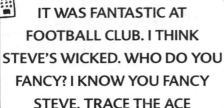

IT WAS FANTASTIC AT FOOTBALL CLUB. I THINK STEVE'S WICKED. WHO DO YOU FANCY? I KNOW YOU FANCY STEVE. TRACE THE ACE

Tracey, I don't fancy anyone!!! I only went to see if they'd let me play. It's inequality not having girls on the team!!! Mandy

Hiya Dave, Thanks for giving me your number. It was brilliant, wannit, at the Club. I didn't know you wuz that good. Steve.

Well I am. And you're not so bad. Dave.

Friday October 5th

Kate, what's up? What you crying for? Why don't you tell me? love from Mandy

I can't Mandy. luv from Kate

Wait for me after school, though. Don't go off on your own again. loads of love, Mandy.

Hi, Dave. Did my head in, school today. Nearly always does, except footie of course. That Tracey's a laugh though. What you doing this weekend? Fancy a kick round the Rec? Steve.

Yeah, ace. When?

Tomorrow morning. About ten?

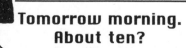

14

Yeah, ace. See you.

Shall I come round, call for you?

Ace. About ten.

HI AGAIN MANDY. ARE WE GOING TO BE BEST FRIENDS? I DON'T KNOW WHY YOU BOTHER WITH KATE ABIDAYA. I THINK SHE'S A WASTE OF TIME. SHE'S ALWAYS GROUCHY. SHE NEVER HAS A LAUGH. NOT LIKE STEVE, HE'S WICKED. DO YOU THINK SO? WILL YOU MEET ME TOMORROW NIGHT? TRACE THE ACE

No, I can't come out at all tomorrow – our cat has to go to the vet.

15

HI STEVE, DO YOU FANCY COMING ROUND TOWN TOMORROW? TRACE THE ACE

Get lost. Steve.

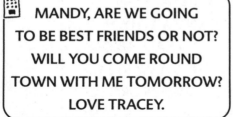
I mean it, Mum. I HATE this house since Dad left. Why can't you two sort things out and think about me for a change. Your daughter who you seem to have forgotten about, Kate

MANDY, ARE WE GOING TO BE BEST FRIENDS OR NOT? WILL YOU COME ROUND TOWN WITH ME TOMORROW? LOVE TRACEY.

No, Tracey. I can't come round town, my auntie's coming.

WHAT A PAIN. I'VE GOT STACKS OF AUNTIES BUT I ALWAYS VANISH WHEN THEY COME ROUND. THEY'RE HERE ALL THE TIME. THAT'S WHY I NEVER AM! WHAT ABOUT US BEING BEST FRIENDS? TRACE THE ACE

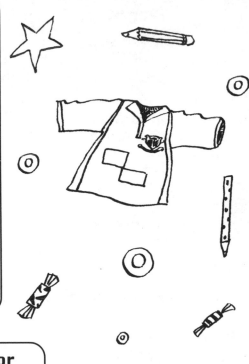

My Auntie Jo's really really nice. She can't come often because she lives in London but we have lots of fun when she does. Got to run, going to the train station with Mum. Over and out and switched off now for ALL weekend. Mandy

You alright for tomorrow? Steve

Yeah. Ace. Dave

Saturday October 6th

That was well pukka, mate. You were really great. Woz you on a team at your old school? Steve.

Yeah. I woz captain last year. Dave

17

Year 5?

Yeah.

Captain of school team?

Yeah.

Well pukka!

Monday October 8th

WILL YOU WALK ROUND WITH ME AT BREAK TODAY, MANDY? LOVE FROM TRACEY

What's up with you!! Are you mad? Do you realise what time it is? I can't even open my eyes this time of day!!!!

Dear Kate, Shall we let Tracey Bellman come round with us at break? love from Mandy.

Dear Mandy. No. Kate

18

Tuesday October 9th

Dear Ms,

Thank you for your letter
and for saying <u>all</u> <u>that</u> about my <u>writing</u>.
I never thought about it being good before!
I thought writing was just writing.

No, that's not it, because I know
Mandy's is horrible
and that's not being bitchy either,
it's just true.

She's my Very Best Friend is Mandy.
She was the only one
at school or at home
who stuck by me when Dad left us.

Well, he didn't leave <u>me</u>
he left my mum
but because of his job
he'll have to come for me later.

I quite like getting letters from you.
I don't get many,

well, none at all really,
just some from my dad

but he can't write often,
he's dead busy.
He's had to do
this rubbish job
because he couldn't get work in acting.

I think it's terrible
the way people get pushed round
if they're out of work!

a bit mad (angry-mad, not off my head)

Kate

PS Actually, I'm thinking
of changing my name to Aimee.

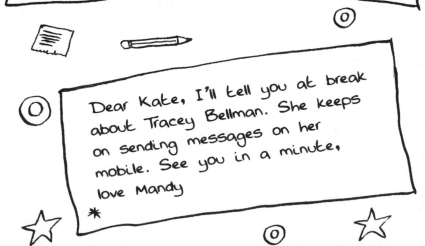

Dear Kate, I'll tell you at break about Tracey Bellman. She keeps on sending messages on her mobile. See you in a minute, love Mandy

Dear Mandy, Break! I can't wait. Did you see poor Dave's face when Ms said to stay behind? I hope he's not in trouble. And I hope you're not going to spend all the time now going on about that Bellman cow. luv Kate

Tuesday October 9

Dear Ms,

Of course I can keep a secret.
Promise.
When you write back
will you tell me who it is?
Write back tomorrow please.
And if I can write about soccer
in these letters and nothing else
that's not so bad.
My dad doesn't think much of women.
It's him says they can't play soccer.
Or do anything much except nag.

Waiting for the Secret Name

Dave Helston

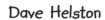

Dear Mum, It was Football Club after school and everyone except me could go. Plus, everyone I know has mobiles and I'm sick of you saying we can't afford things. You're dead tight.
Your Neglected and Bored Out Of My Mind In This House Daughter.

Hiya, Dave

Hi. How you doing?

Great. And so was Soccer Club. You were brilliant. Wish I could play like that.

Thanks. You're ace too.

Wish we had Football Club every day.

Me too. Cool. Dave.

See that Mandy trying to get a game again. Who does she think she is? Girls!

Yeah, girls! Only some of them are not half bad, you know.

Like Kate Abidaya? Seen you eyeing her up.

Get lost.

That Tracey's a laugh, in't she! Turning up on pitch in flowery shorts.

Pity she's got legs like tree trunks!

You'd think they'd kit her out better at home. She's like a walking marquee. AND.... (wait for it!) She fancies you.

 Like parrots she does. It's you she's got her beady eye on.

Parrots? You're weird, man.

Hey, parrots are ace.

I believe you.

Thursday October 11th

Kate, it's not true what you said at break. You're my best friend. Tracey Bellman's stupid. love from Mandy

Mandy Thwaite, Do not send me any more notes. Kate Abidaya.

Thursday October 11

Dear Ms

What's wrong?
You usually put an answer in right away.

Why haven't you written
and told me who your cousin is?
A bit fed up
with all this hanging about
but everything else is starting to get Ace

Yours sincerely

David Helston

Thursday, October 11th

Dear Ms,

Well, I got the name Aimee
from my fave magazine.
I didn't know it meant that.
Ugh! Can you imagine being in love
with any of the boys in our class!
They're feeble!
Most of them stink.
Don't you think so?

Well you probably wouldn't.
After all, it's your job
but I don't know how you put up with them.

24

I wouldn't.
But I'm getting a job in fashion.
I'm very ambitious I am.

I'm going to get on in my life
and do very well.

No messing about for me, I can tell you!

Kate ~~Olivia~~ Abidaya

PS I've scratched my middle name out.
No one must ever know it.
It's from Shakespeare
which my dad used to read a lot.
Mum says he fancied himself as a poet.
She says that's why he left us.
I think about him all the time.
Why couldn't he have taken me?

I hate it at home.

PS 2
I never usually talk about my dad
so please don't say anything about him
in front of the others.

Don't be like this, Kate. You're
my best mate, For Ever. I didn't
even go round at the weekend
when Tracey said.

Get lost Mandy. It's doing my head in, stuff at home, now this. your ex-friend Kate

I'm sorry, Kate. I never knew. I thought it was all sorted at home. I'm really sorry. Tracey's stupid. She could never be my Very Best Friend like you!!! Please be friends again. Loads of love, Mandy

I know she's stupid, stupid. Just like my mum, only she's got Mad Cow Disease. Yes, alright then, we'll still be friends. luv from Kate.

Stupid, me?? Not like her!!!! Honestly! It was really really funny. I told her our cat had to go the vet's and she was talking about Saturday night!!! (I felt a bit mean, after). from your Best Friend In The Universe Mandy Thwaite

Mandy, I'm glad you're my Best Friend and everything's alright again. You shouldn't feel mean about Tracey, she is sooooo stupid. I'm sorry I was so stinky. I wish I could have a mobile but Mum is DEAD TIGHT. luv from Kate your Best Friend in all the Galaxies.

What we doing at half-term? D'you think your mum'll let you come round? loads of love Mandy T.

Dear Mandy T. Don't know. I'll try. It's going to be horrible being home every day. I wish I could move out. luv Kate

Mum, I just HATE you. EVERYTHING'S going wrong and it's all your fault. I think you should see the doctor or the vet. Kate

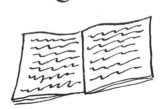

Friday October 12th

Dear Kate,
I'm sorry you were so sad again at break. Why don't you tell Ms? She's really really kind and knows about all sorts. I think she ✳ might help. loads of love M.

Dear Kate, I don't know. But you should tell someone, ✳ loads of love M

Dear M. How can she help? Kate

Anyone know a good vet? Kate

Look, ask your mum again about coming round at half-term. She might change ✳ her mind. M

I wish she'd change planets. K

27

Hi, school wuz even more boring today, wannit. Wish we had footie every day. Steve.

 Yeah, be ace.

Feel like coming round tomorrow? Only prob might be our Jez, my brother. He's a pain. Steve

Be ace, only what time coz me and me dad go watching Leeds every week.

Fantastic! Up the Whites! Play! Play! Play! Score! Score! Score! Top of the League Leeds!

No contest Leeds v. Everton! Everton's the greatest. Only Dad never wants to go now. He says it's too far. Everton! Everton! Ace! Ace! Ace!

Everton? Finger down my throat! Can you come after the match tomorrow? Steve.

Yeah, cool. Thanks.

You can have your tea here, Mum says. Can your dad drop you off? My mum'll take you home later (dead late). Steve

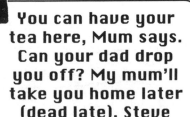 

28

Saturday October 13th

Dear Dad,

Do you like this notepaper?
I bought it specially to send.
I went into town with Mum today.
She won't let me go with Mandy,
my best friend.

I don't have your proper address.
I don't think this one can be right
because last time you didn't reply.
It's dead miserable here since you left.

I hope you're alright.
I miss you lots.
I've not had a letter from you for months.

I bought this paper with cupcakes
because it reminded me of the holidays.
Do you remember me and you making
them in the kitchen and the sun coming in?

   your loving daughter Kate.

PS Mum doesn't know about this.
She'd go bananas if she did.
She goes bananas at everything these
days.

My mum's gone bananas
yum, yum, yum.
My mum's Ape Woman
with a bright red bum!

HI, I'M GLAD I SAW YOU
IN TOWN THIS AFTERNOON
MANDY. WICKED. I'LL NOT SAY
ANYTHING BITCHY ABOUT
KATE IF YOU'LL BE MY FRIEND
AS WELL AS HERS. TRACEY.

Alright. But
don't forget, Kate's
my Very Best
Friend. Mandy

WICKED. SO ME AND
YOU'S FRIENDS. WILL
YOU MEET ME
TOMORROW? TRACEY.

No I can't.
Sorry but we
always have a
day all together
Sundays. Mandy.

WHO DOES?

My family.

30

AW, TRY AND MEET US, MANDS. I NEVER HAVE OWT TO DO, SUNDAYS. EVERYBODY HERE'S ALWAYS GOT HANGOVERS. TRACEY.

Don't call me Mands. I really really hate it. I'm sorry about tomorrow. But it's a family agreement. Mandy.

I DIDN'T KNOW FAMILIES HAD RULES. TRACEY.

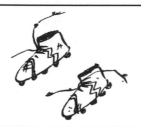

I didn't say rules. I said agreements. And that's we do in my family. That's why I like having my family.

I WISH I LIKED MINE.

Sunday October 14th

Dear Mum,
This might be the last communication I send you. You can't keep treating me like a child. I need some friends. Why won't you let me go to Mandy's? What do you have against her family? I think you're jealous because they're happy. But it's not fair making me as unhappy as you. It's mean and cruel. I hate you and I hate my dad. I'm fed up being nice to you both. I wrote to him but I'll never ever write again. You can tell him. I HATE YOU BOTH. Kate

Hi, Dave. Sorry about our Jez last night. Told you he's a pain, never stops yackin, but it woz great you coming round.

Your Jez is ace. Wish I had a brother like him, Dave.

You're not serious!!!Steve

No. I'm only ever serious about footie and burgers. Dave.

Monday October 15th

Monday October 15th

Dear Ms,

I don't really know what my dad's doing now but he's an actor.

He didn't have poems published
when he left us.
I don't know what he's doing now.

No, Mum doesn't know I want to be in fashion.
She wants me to concentrate on my science.

That's because she thinks
you get fantastically good jobs.

But Mandy Thwaite's dad's unemployed
and he did science.
It's dead good at Mandy's house
even though her dad's not got a job.

They laugh and have a bit of fun,
everyone, all the family.

My mum says they're a disgrace,
all those children and no work.

But she thinks everything's a disgrace
if it's a bit untidy, not washed its face
and wears charity shop jeans.
It's not their fault.

Everyone's just happy at Mandy's.
And they're always making stuff.
I'm not allowed.

Well, Mum never actually says
but there's all kinds of ways
she puts me off!
I think she'd be happier if I left.

    very miserable

        Kate Abidaya

HI MANDY, DID YOU SEE STEVE KEEP STARING AT ME TODAY? TRACE THE ACE

  No, I never noticed. Mandy.

 DO YOU THINK HE FANCIES YOU? I DO. HE'S ALWAYS COMING AND CHATTING YOU UP, ISN'T HE?

Tracey, please stop ringing me. I've got other things to do. And don't be so stupid, please, about Steve. I can talk to someone, can't I, without someone saying he's chatting me up!!! That's very immature, you know. Mandy

Tuesday October 16th

 Kate, I can hardly walk with all that stodge at dinner! Haven't they heard of television cooks!!! love Mandy

They think we're all Fat Ladies. Or Japanese wrestlers. luv Kate

Ugh!!! Honestly, it's going to wreck my training!! I've really really made my mind up to get on the team!!! loads of love Mandy.

Mandy, have you gone mental? luv Kate.

I'm just as good as any of this lot!!! Just look at them! Big-headed morons!!!!!! Mandy

Yeah, but some of them are sweet (xxxx) even if it'll be weeks before we get any sense out of them now with all this football rubbish, luv Kate.

Rubbish? Get a life!!!! We're talking about a dead good game, here. And calling this lot sweet?????? Urgh!!! Can't think where you've been looking!!! As for getting any sense, well, did we ever? M.

35

Hi, Dave. Brilliant about the trials, innit? You're on the team, got to be. Steve.

  Nah, they'll not pick me but I think you've got a dead good chance.

  Nevva!

 What about that Mandy, then?

  What about her?

 Think she stands a chance? For the team, I mean!

  I'd pick her.

Wednesday October 17th

Dear Kate, will you let Tracey come round with us at break? I feel a bit sorry for her. And she IS stupid!!!! Mandy.

Dear Mandy, alright. I feel sorry for her too. As long as you're my Best Friend. Kate.

Dear Ms,

Well, it's my mum.
She never ever stops grumbling.

And she never gets things done,
just moans and complains
ALL THE TIME.

Apart from all her din
it's like a morgue.
She can't stand noise,
brings on her headaches.

I'd love a mobile and a cat
but she says we can't afford one
and she's allergic to animals (all).

I can never have my radio or CDs on,
not even in my bedroom.
Sometimes I think I'll run away.
Even a shop doorway
would be more peaceful.

dead fed-up

Kate

Thursday October 18

Dear Ms,

Magic! Why did you never say before?
My dad says everyone'd be mobbing you
if they knew, asking for his autograph.

My dad won't tell. He promised.
Well, I know I did too
but I tell my dad most things.

It's because when we moved
I'd no mates at first.
I've still not got many.

It's no problem. I'm not bothered.
I never wanted to move.
We always lived in Liverpool before
but when Mum left
Dad got this job up here.

He said it'd be a fresh start
but it's not.
I'm not bothered much.

It's ace about your cousin.
I swear I'll never tell anyone else.
Do you think you could get his autograph?
On a bit of paper'd do.
Only I've got this massive signed poster
of him in my room.

It's not his real signature,
it's from a soccer magazine.

If I had his real one
I could stick that on instead.

And I'd never tell anyone where I got it.
Not if they fastened steel wire
round my neck and kept twisting it
tighter and tighter
or hung me by my ankles
over that big bridge over the river in town
and said they'd drop me on a sewage boat.

Did you know there's more sewage in our rivers
than in any other country in Europe?
It's disgusting.
I might join Greenpeace when I finish school
and do night patrols and combat work.

That's if my dad doesn't get me a job.
He says I should go into I.T. That's the future.
I don't talk to him about Greenpeace.
I've only seen things in his Mail on Sunday.
Greenpeace do a lot of good things I think
even if some people call them terrorists.

I'm sorry about your dog.
We had a dog but Mum took him
when she went.

Funny, that, don't you think
- she left us, me and my dad,
but she took Maxie. He was our dog.

What did yours die of?

    Dave Helston

No one's ever told me a secret before.

Friday October 19th

Dear Ms,

Thank you for talking to me this morning.
It was dead helpful but I do try to understand her
point of view. I've tried and tried but I will try
again at half-term.

    from

    Making Big Efforts To Understand Kate

Dear Kate, see you a week on Monday.
(Boo, hoo!!) I really really wish you
could come round at half-term. I'll miss
you, loads of love, Mandy T. p.s. but we
can always talk on the phone!!!!!

Dear Mandy, I'm GLAD you wrote another note.
It'll cheer me up all next week when there's only me
and the MAD COW MUM in the house and the only
place I get any peace is in the bath. Have you never
noticed how wrinkly I am on Mondays?
You're right, Ms is dead understanding. I think she's
easily the best teacher in this school. (Ms Dead Good
Teacher) luv from Your Very Best Friend, Kate A.
PS please ring me. M.C.M. says we can't afford
to use the phone any more and she throws a
wobbly if she finds out.

HI, MANDY. WA'N'T IT
BORING AT SCHOOL TODAY?
UGH. WILL YOU MEET ME AT
HALF-TERM? LET'S GO FOR A
BURGER OR SOMETHING. I'LL
BUY THEM. TRACE THE ACE

Sorry Trace,
I can't, got soccer
practice all week
with our Dev. He's
really really good
and he's going to
train me for the
school team!!!!

WICKED. CAN I COME AND
WATCH? TRACE THE ACE

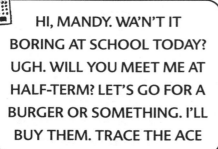

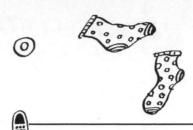

No, we really really need to concentrate. Tell you what though, I'll ring you. I'll try and meet you but I'm not promising. Mandy.

NO, DON'T RING ME. CAN I RING YOU? IT'D BE WICKED, MANDY, IF WE CAN MEET. IN TOWN? THANKS. TRACE THE ACE.

Dave, You'll not forget you're coming round after the game tomorrow? Steve.

No, deffo remember.

Pukka.

Hey, what about Mandy trying to get on the team?

As much chance as you have of getting off with Kate Abi.

Betting?

50p.

Only 50p? Mean parrot.

Who's a pretty boy then?

HI, STEVE. WILL YOU MEET ME IN TOWN TOMORROW, OR SOME OTHER DAY? WE COULD GO SEE A MOVIE. TRACE THE ACE

Sorry, Trace, got a date with an alien.

Saturday October 20th

HI, MANDY. ARE YOU TRAINING TODAY? TRACEY

Hiya, yes, most of the afternoon. Then we're going round to see friends.

Hi, Dave, wuz an ace morning, wannit. What a shot! You're deadly.

Hi, Steve. Ace. How about you? Fastest legs in the west!

D'you fancy playing again tomorrow?

I sure do, dude!

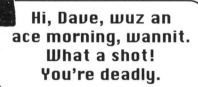

You come here?
Unless the thought of
seeing our Jez again
puts you off. Ugh.
What a mess!

Nah, be great.
Even Jez.

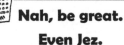

Sunday October 21st

HI, MANDY. I KNOW IT'S
YOUR FAMILY ALTOGETHER
DAY BUT I WISH YOU COULD
MEET ME. JUST HALF AN HOUR?
PLEASE.

Sorry, Tracey.
We've got things
to do here.

I WON'T TEXT AGAIN
TODAY. PROMISE. ONLY, WILL
YOU MEET ME TOMORROW?
WE COULD MEET IN THAT NEW
SHOP NEXT TO COBBLES CAFF,
HAVE A LAUGH. IT'S HORRIBLE
HERE. TRACEY.

I hope
you keep your
promise!!! Don't
ring again! Alright,
I'll meet you in
the new shop, half
past one. Alright?
You don't need
to reply!!

AW, THANKS, MANDY. WICKED! SEE YOU TOMORROW, HALF PAST ONE IN THAT NEW SHOP NEXT TO COBBLES CAFF. SHALL WE GO IN AND HAVE A BURGER OR A HOT DOG? I'LL PAY. TRACE THE ACE.

Monday October 22nd

Cool game, Dave. You're playing great!

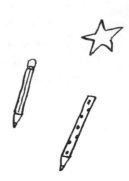

Not so bad, yourself, man! And how about Mandy? Whew, she's fast! Dave

Not just fast! If she doesn't get on the team there's no justice! Steve.

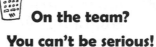

On the team? You can't be serious!

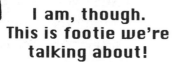

I am, though. This is footie we're talking about!

That's why I'm scared! You had your head invaded or summat?

45

Hey, this is the 21st century! We've had a woman prime minister!

My gran always used to moan about her. Reckoned she was worse than a real man.

You know what I'm saying.

HI, MANDY. THAT WAS WICKED. BEST BURGERS ANYWHERE AND THE BEST DAY I'VE HAD ALL YEAR! SHALL WE GO AGAIN NEXT WEEKEND? TRACE THE ACE.

Hi, Mandy. Great seeing you today. Steve.

Yeah, you, too.

What were you doing out with that moron?

Aw, don't be like that. You know, she's got a load of little brothers and sisters. And she has to look after them because her mum's stoned out of her head most of the time. It's a shame.

46

She tell you that?

 Yes, she did. And I believe her.

 I don't. Things like that don't happen. There's social workers and that.

 She says her dad's away and she thinks he's in prison.

 She's talking porkies! Best keep away!

 HI, AGAIN, MANDY. I KNOW YOU SAID YOU'RE BUSY WITH TRAINING AND STUFF ALL WEEK, BUT I COULD MEET YOU ANY DAY. TRACEY

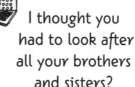 I thought you had to look after all your brothers and sisters?

 I AM, BUT I CAN LEAVE THEM SOMETIMES, CAN'T I?

 On their own?

 MUM'S THERE.

 No promises.

Tuesday October 23rd

Hi, Dave, thought you wuz coming over!

I am, on my way. Thought a dog in our garden wuz a stray. But it's not. See you in ten.

Ten? You got a bike?

Nah, but I thought I'd run, help me training. And I've got very fast feet!

HI, MANDY, HAVE YOU DONE YOUR TRAINING? HAVE YOU GOT TIME TO MEET? I'LL BUY YOU SOMETHING.

It's a bit late, Tracey. My mum doesn't let me go out this time of night and besides, I've got things here I want to do.

CAN'T YOU SPARE HALF AN HOUR?

I told you, I can't!!!

48

Wednesday October 24th

HI, MANDY, I HOPE YOU'RE UP. I WANTED TO ASK YOU SOMETHING.

Tracey Bellman!!!! Don't you have clocks in your house?

SORRY, MANDY. BUT I WANTED TO CATCH YOU BEFORE YOU WENT TRAINING.

You have. You've caught me before I've even got dressed.

MANDY, IT'S REALLY HORRIBLE HERE. MY MUM WON'T GET UP AND THEY'RE ALL MOANING AT ME! I'VE DONE STACKS AND STACKS OF TOAST AND MADE A BIG POT OF TEA ONLY I THOUGHT IT'D GIVE ME SOMETHING TO LOOK FORWARD TO IF WE COULD MEET.

When?

WILL YOU? AW, THAT'S WICKED. SHALL WE MEET IN THAT NEW SHOP AGAIN? I'LL BUY YOU SOMETHING.

Alright. Meet you there this afternoon. But only if you promise not to buy me anything.

WICKED, MANDY. CAN I BUY YOU A BURGER?

No, I'll buy my own if I want one. 3PM alright with you?

Hi, Steve. You seeing Dave again tomorrow?

Hiya, Mandy. Yeah, we're having a kick round on the Rec.

Can you come round here after?

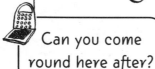

I'll try.

Steve, it's really really important.

Alright. You on the Ormrod Estate?

Yeah. 23 Fellbeck Terrace.

50

Thursday October 25th

Hiya, Steve.
Ace, this morning. But
you raced off too fast
(you're not as fast as
me, though!) to fix up
owt for tomorrow.

Yeah, Mandy
rang.

And?

She wanted to
tell me summat so
I went round. It's
that Tracey again.
Sounds a reet mess.

Tracey is a
mega-mess!

Nah, this might
be serious.
She's been telling
Mandy things about
stuff at home. I
promised I'd not tell.

S'alright.

You'll be first
I tell when Mandy
says it's alright.

51

When Mandy says!

And Mandy believes her?

I wouldn't.

What's she gonna do? Mandy, I mean?

And is she doing?

It's serious, Dave. Mandy thinks Tracey might get put in care if it's all true.

Yeah.

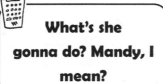

That's what I said too and Mandy says she wasn't sure at first but now she's dead sure what Tracey says is straight.

I said she should tell her mum and dad. I can't think of owt else.

I think so. I said I'd ring her tomorrow morning, see what's going on.

What about footie, then?

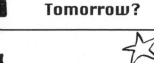
Tomorrow?

Yeah.

Meet on t'Rec, ten o'clock?

Ace.

Saturday October 27th

Hi, Mandy. You alright?

Hi, Steve. Yeah. Thanks for phoning.

How d'you get on?

Well, my dad was going round on his own. Then Mum said it'd be better if they both went. Just in case.

In case?

And was Tracey in?

Well, in case Mrs Bellman tried anything on. You know.

No. I'm really really glad, too. I feel terrible for telling but I was scared about what might happen. Tracey's not old enough for all that.

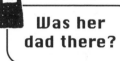 Was her dad there?

No, what Tracey said is true, I think. Look, can you come round? It's a bit complicated.

 Hi, Steve. Where wuz you today? I was ringing all avvie. Dave.

Hiya. I wuz at Mandy's. She rang, wanted me go over.

 And you went!

It's a reet mess. Mandy's mum and dad went to Tracey's. Tracey wasn't in but her mum was. Stoned out her head. Only promise you'll not tell.

 Course I'll not.

Not anyone! It's dead serious.

Sunday October 28th

Hi, Steve. Ace, that game, wannit. Some of your mates are not bad. Nearly as good as my old mates in Liverpool.

At least twice as good!

All right, I'll be honest. This lot's as good as some of our Year 4s were!

Never be as good as you at telling porkies, though!

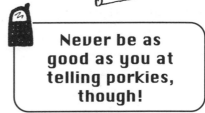

I'm ace at everything I have a go at!

Aw yeah!

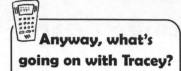 **Anyway, what's going on with Tracey?**

 I don't know, but Mandy's mum and dad went to the police.

 They nevva!

 What else could they do?

 Aw, you should keep away from the busys.

Even when it's little kids involved?

 I dunno, Steve.

Mum, I wish you'd never told me. I wish I hadn't been born. Why did you and dad have me if you were going to do this to me? Kate Olivia Abidaya

Monday October 29th

Mum, I might never speak to you again so don't expect me to. After school I might go to Mandy's. Kate

Dear Ms,

Mum told me last night she's getting a divorce.
From my dad.

I locked myself in my room
and cried all night.
I'm dead sad.
I don't understand why she's doing this.
I don't know what Dad'll say.

When you're divorced, that's it.
They'll never get back together now.

desperately unhappy Kate

Dear Kate, was it alright, yesterday?
You said when I rang you'd try and ring
back. What happened? Love Mandy

Horrible. Too bad to
talk about. Kate.

Will you tell me after
school? Please. It's best
if you share something.
loads of love, Mandy

I don't know. I'll try.
luv Kate. PS And thanks

57

Hi, Steve, Mandy here.

Hiya. You alright?

Yeah, only I want to talk to you.

Tracey again?

No, Kate.

Aw, no!

Steve, I wouldn't bother if it wasn't really really urgent. You know I don't fuss!!!

Alright, only don't you think you should tell Ms or your mum? Why me?

Ms knows, Kate told her. She says Ms was wonderful. And I have told Mum. She thinks it might help if someone else knows, someone in our class, someone I can trust.

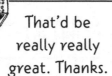
That'd be really really great. Thanks.

D'you want me to come round?

(0)

Tuesday October 30th

Tuesday October 30

Dear Ms,

Ace! That's well good.
Course I don't mind waiting,
I'm good at waiting, got medals for it.

I don't ever get to see my cousins
either and I don't write to them.
No one in our family writes letters.

I wish one of my cousins
was famous like yours.

I never knew animals had heart attacks.
Seems funny that.
I think that's what my grandad had.
But I never see my family
so I can't ask.

I never said Greenpeace were terrorists
but I know some people do.
I'm going to ask Steve's brother
what you have to do
to be a member. He's ace.

Before we moved
I went to Computer Club every Wednesday
but there's nothing here
just Football Club and that's only once a week.
It'd be ace if we had it every day.

They have Computer Club at Valley Road.
Did you know?
My dad's brilliant on computers
but we've not got one now.
He says he'll get me one if I want.
For Krimble.

D'you think you'll get another dog?
I'd like one.

looking forward to that autograph
and sworn to deadly secrecy

Dave Helston

Dear Kate, I'm sorry about what you told
me about your mum and dad. It must be
really really terrible. I hope you like this card
I made you. Your Very Best Friend, Mandy.

Hi, Steve, thanks for coming round last night.

That's O.K.

Thanks for not telling anyone else.

Told you, I'm fantastic at secrets.

You were really really great today with Kate. She's a lot more cheerful, isn't she?

Yeah, I think so.

I feel really really sorry for her. But at least her mum's not like Tracey's.

Yeah, poor old Trace the Ace!

Thursday November 1st

Dear Ms,

I'm feeling a lot better in some ways
but totally confused.
Grown-ups do your head in,
they tell you one thing
and then they do another.
All the time!
When Dad left
Mum said I'd always have her.
(Big deal)

But she acts
as though she can't stand
having me around!

And nobody ever asked what _I_ wanted.
If they had
I'd have gone with my dad.

I tried to talk to her, like you said.
To find out about the divorce.
Then I asked her not to do it.

She says she's got to.
It's ruining her life!
But what about mine?

totally uncared about

Kate

PS I am interested in what you said
about computers.
But it's not easy being interested
in anything much, now.

PS 2 It's a good job I've got friends.

Dear Kate, I think it's exciting
about these computers. Have you
changed your mind about that
competition? There's still time.
Loads of love, M.

Dear M (cool) Alright. I'll try,
but it's down to you if I make a
real prat of myself, luv Kate.

Dear K, you won't!!! loads
of love, Mands.

**Hi, Mandy.
Any news?**

Hiya, Steve.
What about?

**Well about Kate or
about Tracey or about
your secret training
schedule.**

No news about
Tracey except
people are saying
she'll never come
back to Waterside.
Kate's still really
really unhappy but
she's writing a poem
for the competition.
And my training's
not secret. Any top
class athlete could
do it!!!!

Tuesday November 6th

Tuesday November 6

Dear Ms,

Thanks for all that stuff on Greenpeace.
I've read a lot and my dad started reading it too.
He says newspapers twist things sometimes.

I'm not talking about you
but my dad says
it's the same with women.

I wish we could see my mum some time
but we never even talk about her,
just don't.

I'm looking forward to that news
about computers. Everyone is.

Well, all the lads.
And maybe that Mandy is, and Kate, too.
Did you know one of Mandy's brothers
had trials for Leeds?
Your cousin might have heard of him.

He didn't get picked
but I think it's ace anyway, that.
I hope I get trials for Everton some day.

I never asked my dad about another dog.
I suppose he might, he liked our Maxie.
But I'd like one a bit smaller this time.

I think I'd have a pit bull.

Our Maxie never knew when to stop growing,
my gran said. She said he'd feet like an elephant
when he was a puppy and that's a sign, deffo.

I've tried phoning her sometimes since we moved.
My dad doesn't know.
But she doesn't like the phone.

I suppose that's why she doesn't answer.
She would have if she'd known it was me.

She's dead funny, my gran, makes you laugh.
She always had brilliant jokes,
even my dad laughed at her jokes.

He can't stand it though,
when I talk about them all.
It's because of my mum, see.

Dave Helston

Dear Ms,

I do try to understand!
That's why I asked her to talk.
She never tries to understand me.

I'm sorry
but I don't want
to talk about her any more.

fed-up with writing letters

fed-up with life

Kate Abidaya

67

Friday November 9th

Friday November 9th

Dear Ms,

Thank you for talking to me on Tuesday.
It helped a lot. I told Mum what you said
and for once she listened, then we talked.

We had a long talk last night and for once she
wasn't all moany-moany and head-achey.

I think she was really trying to understand
(she's got a lot of trying to do before she gets
anywhere near) but she did listen and (are you
listening, because this is amazing?) Mandy's
having a sleepover and Mum says I can go.
Incredible. In summer Andrea Summersgill had
one and invited me but Mum wouldn't let me go.

feeling quite cheerful

Kate

Saturday November 10th

Saturday November 10th

Dear Gran,

How're you doing?
I'm settling down here
and got some good mates.
Steve especially.
We play footie together.
I've telephoned a few times.
I hope you'll write back.
I've got some fantastic things to tell you.
I keep thinking I'll try and get a dog.
I miss our Maxie.
I miss you too, Gran.

Yours, David

Monday November 12th

Dear Kate, it was really really wonderful having you sleep over. Did you enjoy it? loads of love, Mandy

Dear Mandy, it was perfect. I wish I had a family like yours. Your dad's daft, I think he's goofy and wonderful. love from your Best Friend Ever Kate

Tuesday November 13th

Dear Mandy,
Congratulations
again. I'd be dead
scared if it was
me. How do you
feel? luv Kate

Dear Kate, Thanks, again!!
I feel great, really really
wonderful. Amazed!!! And
glad they've picked the very
best players for the team,
for once!!! from your Very
Best Mate, M.

Tuesday November 13th

Dear Ms,

It's fantastic, innit?
Me on the team.
Yeah!

My dad says my luck's changed
but I like what you said too
about me getting back what I've put in.

Coz I've really tried this term.
It's fantastic, innit?
Oh, I've put that twice.

I'm trying different words to ace after what
you said about English and rich language.

I've put fantastic in a letter to my gran too.
That'll give her a surprise
- not the bit about the team
(she'll be amazed about that
but I want to keep that for when I see her).

What I meant was my letter.
I wrote to her on Saturday
before the match.
I hope she sends one back.

I miss my gran.

It wasn't her fault Mum left us.
She wasn't to blame
but the way Dad goes on you'd think it was.

She always liked my dad, Gran did.
But he wouldn't listen to me
so he didn't tell her when we left.

That's why
she's not got in touch.
She doesn't know where I am.

Yeah, I think I would like a pit bull
or an Alsatian but they're too big.
Pit bulls are ace.

But maybe I'd not have much time
to take it for walks
now I'm on the team.

Did you know we practise every day?

          keeping that secret for ever

              Dave Helston
                      Soccer Star

PS don't tell anyone I said that

Tuesday November 13th

Dear Ms,

Isn't it funny how some boys
are always talking about football,
as if nothing else existed in life?

It's a good thing we've got
the computers to talk about too.
Have you got any news?

Yes, I would like to be involved.
It would be good practice
for when I leave school.
And I enjoy computers.

I'm going to Art College.
I'm going to be either in Fashion
or in some sort of Design.

Mandy's sleepover was cool.
Me and Mandy talked all night!
I told her about Mum and Dad.

I was talking to her mum next day.
She's really great. She told me that
her sister-in-law (Mandy's Auntie Jo)
went to Art College.

She says next time they go to Mandy's Auntie Jo's I can go too. Mandy said she wants to go next week.

Fashion-Queen Kate

PS I'm quite enjoying trying to write a poem for the competition. I think it'll be quite short. Is that alright?

PS 2 It's dead good about Mandy, isn't it?
Being on the team, I mean.
She's not like the boys, though,
always talking about football
and nothing else
or always talking about herself,
like they do.

Hi, Mandy, brilliant, innit? I couldn't stop grinnin when old Harding announced it. Congratulations. D'you fancy celebratin?

Hiya, Steve. Thanks. I'm still grinnin!!! I hope we can celebrate. I'll see what Mum and Dad think coz they've already said we'll have a big family celebration Sunday. M

Any news about Tracey?

No, I asked Ms at home-time but she doesn't know, either and I've tried and tried Tracey's mobile but it's switched off.

 You think she thieved it, that phone? Coz what everybody's saying is they're dead poor and her dad's in the nick.

He is and they are!!! But Tracey bought that mobile herself. She showed me the receipt!!!

How'd she manage that?

Well, she used to keep a bit of her paper-round wage back, every week for ages till she had enough. No one at home knew she had it. She kept it secret, she said they'd rob it to sell if they knew.

 Poor old Trace.

Hi, Steve, what about this, then? How bad can things get? A girl on the team. I might not play. Dave.

 Aw, come off it. Don't be a soft-head all your life. You and Mandy's the two best players this school's got. Probably the best two it's ever had and you're talking about wrecking it. Don't be a dinosaur.

A dinosaur? I'm gonna be a Giant, me. You see that game last night, San Francisco Giants on their new ground? Ace. Bet they don't have any players called Mandy!

Their loss! And I didn't see t'game, we've not got Sky. But I'm telling you, this final'll be ace too, you and Mandy on t'same team. Be honest, don't you think she's amazin?

 I know you do.

She's alright.

Dear Mandy, I wrote this last night. It's for you.
I hope you like it. Please don't show it to anyone
else when I'm there. luv from your Very Best
Friend for ever and ever Kate.

Some Friends

Some friends are cool
but all they talk about is trendy clothes
and telly
and should they get a nose-ring
or one for on their belly.

Some friends are ace
but all they think about is boys
and putting make-up on their face
and should they diet
until they get so skinny there's a riot.

Some friends are like my friend
who is funny and fantastico
she plays football better than Beckham,
and listens when you need her.
No wonder she's so popular.

by Kate Abidaya

for her Very Best Friend Mandy

Dear Kate, thanks for my pressie-poem. It's really really brilliant. Thank-you!!! I've never had a poem before!!! loads and loads of love, Mandy p.s Clever-clogs, you!!!!

Hi, Steve.

Mandy, how're you doing? Can you still stand up after all that training?

Better than ever. Ha'n't you noticed I've grown twenty centimetres this week!!!!

Thought we'd got a giraffe in Year 6!

Pack it in!!! I did have an invitation for you. Might not bother now, we don't want any smartarses round our house.

Invitation? Aw, go on!

Well, we're having a party this Sunday for me getting on the team. Just my family, really, but I'm asking Kate. And Mum and Dad said you can come. If you want.

Pukka. Do you want me to come?

I wouldn't have said, would I? Well?

 Yeah, I'll come. Thanks. What time?

 About two. Sort of instead of dinner and going on to about seven o'clock, Dad said. He'll run you home, or our Dev will.

Friday November 16th

Dear Kate, we're having a party on Sunday to celebrate me getting on the team. Can you come? Please!!!!!!!! loads of love, M.

Yes. I'll come. Whatever anyone says. You asking anyone else? luv Kate

Naw, just me Very Best Friend. Oh, and Steve. loads of love, M.

*

Ooooh.

Hi, Steve. See you tomorrow?

Course. Gotta keep on our toes (ha, ha).

Sunday November 18th

Hi, Mandy, that wuz well pukka.

Hiya!! Cool, wannit?

Your Dev's fantastic. I'd seen him play footie but never knew he could do guitar like that. Wish I could play like that. Top of the Pops! Well cool.

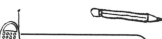

You wouldn't think so if you lived here!!! Dad says they're gonna soundproof the basement in spring. Roll on spring!!!!!!

Monday November 19th

Dear Mandy, it was the most totally brilliant party I've ever been to. The best party possible. Honestly, you're dead lucky. I think your Dev's gorgeous. luv Kate

Dear Kate, Thanks about the party, but not about Dev!!!! He's alright, I suppose. Have you ever seen Steve's brother? Now he is
* gorgeous!!!!! love M

Thursday November 22nd

Dear Ms

It's been brilliant this week,
all that training.

No one else'll stand a chance.
Well, they might, but I think we're better
and fitter than any school for miles.
I think we're even better than Tennyson Avenue,
my old school.
And faster.
I think we play great as a team now.
That's cool.
Even with Mandy on the team.
Well (never tell anyone I said this) especially
with Mandy on the team. She's ace.

I've still not had a letter back from my gran
but it's not been long enough
and anyway
she'll have to go and buy stamps and stuff.

       Dave Helston
         (who's bringing new life
           to the Waterside Team)

Thursday November 22nd

Dear Ms,

I don't believe how miserable
you can feel after being so cheerful.

It's sadder than Bambi at my house.

Mum's been seeing a solicitor.
She's getting headaches again all the time.

She grumbles if I leave the doors open.
She grumbles when I shut them.

I can't do anything right.

I'm going to ask Mandy's mum
if I can live there!

Mandy's got a mobile and personal CD player!
Nearly everyone has a mobile except me.

                    totally fed-up with everything
                     except sometimes at school
                         and being with Mandy

                Kate Unhappy Abidaya

PS Mandy's asking her mum
if I can stay there at the weekend.
There'll be no other friends,
just me – her very best one.

PS 2 I ripped my poem up.
It was too short and dead boring anyway
but Mandy says it's good so I'm writing
it out again. I do quite like it
but it's hard believing it,
even though I've written it.

Friday November 23rd

Dear Kate, I'm really really relieved your mum says
you can come tomorrow.
Bring your new CD. You're
really lucky getting that.
None of us have it. loads
of love, M.

Dear M, It's totally ace, innit.
Will Dev be around? Whoops, I
think Ms has her beady eye
on me. Send this later. luv K

Monday November 26th

Dear Ms,

It's ace. Fantastic.
I've stuck the signature over the old one
(which is bigger but not a real one).
It looks dead good.

Steve's coming round tomorrow,
I can't wait to show him.
Did you mean it about me telling the others?
Do you not mind?

Shall I tell them or will you?
I think it's right, though,
like you said.
It's only fair.

My dad says
if you and Mrs Harding want
he'll come after school one day
and help you set up a Computer Club.

He says he'll come in some time
if you like
and give you some advice
because he's ace on computers.

I've still not got a letter from my gran.

I've sent off to Greenpeace
for some information
but I can't be a member.
It costs too much.

My dad says you don't have to be
a member of an organisation
to support what they do.
I could go on a march or something.

Did you think about that pup?
What will you call it?
How about Eric?
I'm deffo not getting one.

Soccer-crazy Dave

Monday November 26th

Dear Ms,

It was fantastic being at Mandy's.
We had a good laugh
and she showed me her family photographs.
A lot of them are artists and things like that.

She said her uncle's a writer.
A lot of times he's got no work.
Like my dad!

But Mandy says her uncle always
gets jobs in pubs
and places like that, near home.

I suppose some people can.
Dad can't.

I was talking to Andrea Summersgill today.
She says she's got lots of last year's
fashion magazines, the dead expensive ones.
Her mum buys them.
Andrea says she'll lend me them.

I'm going round after school.
I've not told Mum.
She'll not notice.

The boys in our class make me sick.
Anyone would think
the whole world was an enormous football.

I suppose if it was,
Dave Helston would think he could
kick it round the moon and back!
He thinks he's totally fantastic.

Andrea says he fancies me.
Well I don't fancy him.
Andrea says I'm fussy
but I don't see anything wrong in that.

My dad always used to say
'Think well of yourself, girl.
Nobody else will if you don't!'
(That's what my poem is about).

I'm really trying at home.
It doesn't make much difference though.
Mum's either at work or in bed.
I hardly ever see her.
And she's always got headaches
and crying.
Last night she said it was Dad's fault.

I don't see how it can be.
She's got to sort herself out!
She told me to when Dad left,
told me I was responsible for how I felt.

Well, so is she!
She can't expect me to look after her!

Suffering and not in silence

Kate

PS I am trying.
I make her cups of coffee
and never make a noise
but I'm not stopping in any more
just for her.

Tuesday December 4th

Dear Ms,

I've not got a letter from my gran yet.

Steve Mason thinks that signature's dead cool.
He wouldn't believe it was real at first
but he did after. And he was gobsmacked
when I told him it's your cousin.
I've told all the others today.
I bet you could tell!

It's been ace having a secret with someone
but it's alright now they all know.
It's more fair, innit.

We're good mates, me and Steve.
He says I'm the best thing that's happened
to the school team.
(I think he means second best, really!)

We're both practising like mad for Friday's game.
If we win we're in
(the finals).

I'm going to his on Saturday
and he's coming to the match
with me and my dad.
We go every Saturday.

87

It's not the same not seeing Everton
but Leeds is not bad.

I think there's a few things
not so bad here
and I've been trying to get friends
with some of the girls.

I don't think you should just have boys as friends.
I think that's where my dad went wrong.

The girls here are not so good, though.
They're a bit stuck-up I think.

Dave Soccer-Giant Helston

Tuesday December 4th

Dear Ms,

Your letter was a big help.
And so was our chat.
Well, it might be, if I try out what you said.
And I will. I think I'll start tonight.

I'll try and be more positive, about everything.
Not that she ever is!

Once, I fixed earplugs on the lounge radio
so I could listen to music I liked.
But she said she didn't like them,
said it made her feel isolated.
(It was great, isolated away from her.)

I'm going to ask her
if I try amazingly hard to be helpful
and not to be noisy when she's not well
(I never, ever am)
if she'll get me a mobile phone.

I know she's not got me anything
for Christmas yet,
so she might get me one.

So I'll write again next term
and I hope you have
a totally incredible time at Christmas.
I'm going to. Definitely.

Me and Mandy have promised
to see each other every day in the holiday.
Well, except for Christmas Day and Boxing Day.

All her aunties and uncles go to their house
for a massive get-together.
She's going to ask if I can go.

So it's going to be quite good.
Even if I won't be seeing my dad,
I suppose.

feeling positive,

Kate

PS David Helston doesn't half fancy himself! He keeps grinning at me!

And it's not just me who's noticed, Andrea asked me if I'm seeing him. As if!

Friday December 7th

Hi, Mandy. I'm shattered. Are you? Bet you are. You must be. You wuz well pukka. My dad said you were t'best player on t'field. How about that?

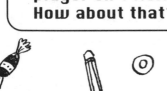

Hiya. Aw, tell your dad thanks. Honestly, though, I'm not really tired. I'm not saying nobody else is fit but our Dev did nearly have my legs off last week!!!! He'd make a killer trainer even for United!!!!

Urgh. Wash your mouth out!

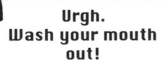

Hi, Steve. Well ace, innit! I never thought I'd get that last goal though. You wuz ace. So wuz Mandy. We wuz all bloody brilliant!

90

Yeah, Waterside For Ever. Well pukka, mate. That last goal wuz amazin!

 Thanks. We practising tomorrer?

Yeah. I'm going round Mandy's later though.

 Warrgh!

Sunday December 9th

Dear Gran,

I hope you got my last letter.
If you didn't you might not get this.
I wish we lived nearer.
I hated it when we moved
but it's not bad now.
Me and my mate Steve play loads of footie.
You could come up here and meet him.
It'd be ace, Gran, if you came.
I've got some brilliant news
but I want to tell you, not write it

love David

Monday December 10th

Dear Ms,

it was great, wannit?
I didn't think you'd be there
but I suppose soccer's in the family,
innit?

We're in the finals now.
No stopping us.
It's about time this school
did something really useful.

Do you think we'll get the cup?
I do.

After school on Friday
I was talking to Mandy Thwaite.
She's alright for a girl.
She and Steve are dead good mates.

I saw her last week,
out shopping after school
-    Mandy and her brothers
and her mum and dad.
They all looked dead happy.

I like Kate Abidaya
but she always looks at me
as if I'm some sort of perv,
as if I've done something terrible
or I smell. And I don't.
You know dead well.

When will we know deffo
about the computers?

If it happens it'll be brilliant.
But I think we should keep it quiet,
we don't want Valley Road finding out
else they might get the money instead.

If we can spend it on new systems,
desktop publishing and that,
we could start a school magazine.

Had you thought what we could do?

I think it'd be well good
if we did something about the
environment.
We could have a green page.
Some of us could interview people in town.

Top Team member

Dave Helston

Monday December 10th

Dear Ms,

This will probably be
my last letter before Krimble.

I put my poem in for the competition on
Friday.
I don't think it stands a chance.
But it was alright writing it. I enjoyed it.

Mum's cheered up
and she's actually promised
she'll buy me a mobile phone.

She says getting divorced
is a positive step.

She hopes I'll see it like that.

She says it doesn't mean she'd ever
stop me seeing Dad. (She couldn't!).
It's just that she wants to start being practical.
She does seem more cheerful.

And she says I can ask Mandy round
any time I want. I don't believe it.
We've still not heard from Dad.
It's ages, over a year now, since I saw him.

I think about him a lot, but after all,
it's Mum who looks after me.

She couldn't help it
if he couldn't get a job acting.

And she works totally hard in that shop,
on her feet morning till night for peanuts.

She does her best, I suppose.

Mandy's got a mum and a dad
to look after her
and her sisters and brothers.

Mum was really pleased
about the computer and the magazine.

So am I. It's dead cool.

I couldn't believe it at first
when you said.
But I'm fantastically glad you did.

David Helston shook my hand
and everyone laughed.

I think I went red
but I don't care.
I think he's cute.

Mum said she was editor
of her school magazine one year.
She never told me that before.

I think being an editor is really cool
and I'm glad Mum remembered.
She's going to ask Granny
if she's still got her copy of the magazine.
She will have.

Granny never throws anything out.
I can't wait.
It'll look ancient,
not like the one we'll have

but it'll be quite exciting
to see Mum's name in print.
Even more when mine is.

Happy Krimble, Ms.

From the First Editor of Waterside's School
Magazine

Kate O. Abidaya

PS Do they have 'firsts'
in the Guinness Book of Records?
I think they do.
Will you enter me?

PS 2. Mum heard from Dad's solicitor today.
She didn't want to spoil my Christmas but felt I had a right to know.
Dad's living abroad.

He won't fight the divorce.

He won't pay Mum any of the money he owes either.

Monday December 13th

 Thursday December 13th

Dear Ms,

My gran didn't write.
I sent her another letter to be sure she got it.

I've been practising every day with Steve
then again with the team.

And it's almost here, the final!
Will you be there?

Me and Steve think
we should start a magazine.
Steve could be the artist.
He's dead good at drawing, isn't he?

His brother's a member of Greenpeace
and he's real cool.
He's seventeen,

next year he goes to university.
My dad says I could go if I wanted.
I don't think so.

Jez (that's Steve's brother)
gave me some of his Greenpeace stuff.
He says they're not terrorists
but I told him I knew that really.

I think it's a good idea if you wait for a dog
till the good weather.

Have you thought about a parrot?
The weather doesn't matter with parrots
and they're fantastic colours.

I saw a film on telly about the Amazon.
There were all these parrots flying.
Brilliant!
Hey - they were - brilliant.
The colours, I mean.
Funny!

I've noticed how when you write words,
sometimes you get jokes like that.
(did you laugh?)

I was thinking of writing a letter
to someone else. So far
I've only ever written to you and my gran.

My dad says if you need a hand with the computers
give him a shout.
He's ace at them.
I think I might get one for Krimbo.
Steve's got some great games
and I could send letters to my gran.

looking forward to Krimbo holidays

Dave
(Waterside's most ~~sensay~~ fantastic star)

PS If I did write a letter to someone else
it might be to one of the girls in our class.

Friday December 14th

Dear Clever Clogs Kate.
Congratulations!!! Honestly,
I'm really really glad.. I
told you it was good!!!!
And it's better than good.
It's a winner!!!! love your
Very Best Friend M
*

Dear M. thanks for
your congratulations. I
don't believe it! Wait
till tomorrow, though.
I'll be congratulating
you. I can't wait to tell
Mum. I think she'll be
quite pleased. luv Kate

Hi, Mandy, you all set for the big game?

Hiya, Steve! I think so. How about you?

Me? I don't need to get ready. I'm always mega fit, me.

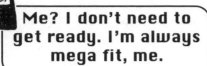

Saturday December 15

Dear Kate,

I was well glad your poem got first prize.
I think it's ace.
I think you are too.
I hope you're at the match
.this avvie coz I'm playing.

A Secret Admirer

Hi, Mandy, you wuz brilliant. Aw, yeah!

Thanks Steve. You were really really great!!! I never realised you were a First Division Dribbler!!! We're having another celebration tomorrow. Honestly, what we like, eh!!!! The Thelebratory Thwaites!!!

100

You what?

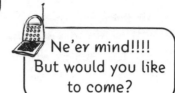

Ne'er mind!!!!
But would you like
to come?

To the Thelebration?

Yeth.

You're on.

Monday December 17th

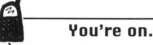

Monday December 17

Dear Ms

********Waterside Forever!********
Yeah. Best thing ever happened to this school.
My dad says my last goal was the best he's
ever seen.

**********Fantastic**********

Why did you never tell us about your degree?
Technology.............brilliant!
What did you want to be a teacher for then?

If I'd been you
I'd not have ended up in a school.

My dad says teaching's a fool's game
because the government's messed it all up
with loads of red tape
and the money stinks.
He says people who can do things get on with it
and those who can't, teach.

I don't think it's right that,
because you can do a lot of things.
And Technology. Great!

You never answered me about a parrot.
I've been thinking about it.
It's not such a good idea.

I'd really like to see those parrots
in the Amazon in real life.
I wouldn't want one in a cage.

They're alright in cages for some people
because they were born in captivity
but I don't think it's right.

Is it right, about the computers, then?
Are we deffo getting them?
Cool!

Do you think we will have a magazine?
I think it'd be brilliant.
I could be editor.

I wouldn't mind
working with some of the girls,
maybe Mandy or Kate.
It's ace, Kate winning the competition.
She deserves it.
I couldn't write a poem if you tied me
to a giant tarantula's web
and threatened to let it at me
unless I wrote a poem!
Could 'HELP' be a poem?

My gran didn't write yet.

My dad's got stand tickets for Saturday's game.
He's taking Steve too.
He says we deserve it for winning the final.

Do you think Mrs Harding
will give us a day off, next term?
It's the first time Waterside's ever won the
trophy, isn't it?

Top Star Dave

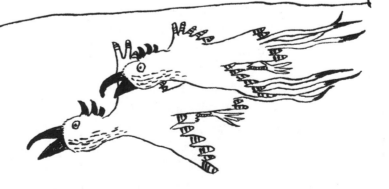

Tuesday December 18th

Congratulations to Kate Abidaya of 6S who won
1st Prize in the annual Year 6 Poetry Competition
Kate's winning poem 'Just Like My Heart'
is printed below.

Other prizewinners are:
2nd Mark Macmillan for 'Donkey'
3rd Gemma Stephenson for 'Noel'
Runner-up Grace Latif for 'Animal Song'

Copies of all the poems will appear in the first issue
of the new school magazine. We hope this will
appear at the end of next term.

Just Like My Heart

One day I found a stone.
It was old, so old.
In the middle was a hole.
I peeped through and saw magic there
beautiful and rare.

That stone was like my heart I know
and though everything is dark
and no one loves me any more
one day I shall find
that magic place again
and peep inside
and hiding there
is all the love I need.
"Oh! You were there all the time!
My own love, just for me
waiting deep inside!"

Tuesday December 18th

Dear Ms,

Best news since the finals,
my gran's sent me a letter and a Krimbo Card.

Dear David,

I was made up to hear from you.
I had flu when your first letter came but it helped me get better.

The first thing I did was get on the bus and head for town to buy
some paper and envelopes. I got a whole book of stamps then I can
write again.

I've not written a letter for donkey's years, not since my dad was at
sea and Mam made us all write every week.
It put us all off writing letters.

It's a shame about Maxie.
Do you think you will get another dog?
You remember your Auntie Belle and Uncle Billie, what a pair of
soft-heads they were about animals? Well just after you left, your Uncle
Billie won the Lottery and they moved to this massive house.
They got it dead cheap. It's down the Dingle. Well, they turned it
into this sort of Rescue Centre.

She did little drawings of Uncle Billie and Auntie
Belle and all my cousins on the back of her letter.

I forgot she was good at drawing.
She's as good as Steve.

I'll show you her drawings.
They're dead funny.
I think she could have made a lot of money.
She could've been a famous cartoonist.
I'll tell her when I write.
I'm going to write to her on Saturday,
after the match.

I go up and give your Auntie Belle a hand when I can. The stories
I could tell! I could write a play for the telly.

I was up there just before I got flu.
Your Uncle Billie looked as if he'd swallowed a snake, wriggling and
squirming all over the place. 'What's up, lad?' I says. 'We got a new
dog in, Margie,' he says, 'and I've just been giving him a tonic. He's
dead run-down. But he's got fleas big as rabbits and they've all
hopped on me!' I kept my distance, I can tell you. Well I'll be going
now and I hope you have a lovely Christmas.
I will get up there one of these days.

Give my best wishes to your dad.
Tell him to keep his head up.
                    love
                          Gran

PS Horatio says Hello!

Horatio's my gran's parrot.
He's dead ancient.
He used to belong to a seaman
and his language is fowl. (Ha! Ha!)
It's great we're having a school magazine.

106

I'm a bit disappointed
about Kate Abidaya being editor
because I thought it would be me
but I'm glad, too
because I like her.

And I'll wait, like you said,
and see what she can do.

I wrote another letter this week (Mega-Secret!)

If you like, next term
we could work together, me and her.
We could share the Environmental Page
and I could do a Sports Page.

We'll have to have one
and me and my dad go every week.
Steve comes with us most times now.
Steve could do cartoons on the Sports Page.

Have a nice Krimbo. See you next term.

Dave

HIYA, MANDY. HOW
ARE YOU? I HOPE YOU'VE
NOT FORGOT ME. TRACEY.

Tracey!! Where
are you? I've tried
and tried to phone
you. Mandy

I KNOW. BUT I'VE HAD IT SHUT OFF IN CASE ANYONE HERE HEARD IT. IT'D BE ROBBED IN A MINUTE!

Where are you?

ON THIS DEAD COOL ISLAND WITH BRIGHT BLUE SEA SPLASHING ROUND MY FEET. I LIVE IN A LITTLE HUT ON THE WHITE SAND. IT'S WICKED, THIS PLACE. TRACE THE ACE

Tuesday December 18th

Dear Ms,

I'm sending this with a broken heart.

You might not read it till next term
but I wanted to tell you something I found out.

On Friday night I knew Mum would be late home
from work and I was rummaging in her bedroom.
I know I shouldn't have
but I've told her now and she says it's alright.
I'll never do it again
but the thing is I found these letters from Dad.

They were horrible.
I didn't know he could be like that.

He left me and Mum for someone else.
And he was seeing her while he was living with us.
And poor Mum knew.
He told her that if she told me
he would never contact me again.
He blackmailed her.
And she kept quiet. For me.

I stayed awake all night.
Then Mum came in.
And we both cried. And talked and talked.
And I think I understand but it does my head in.

I won't hate Dad.
But I think Mum's been dead brave.
And we're going to have a Dead Good Krimble.

Anyway, I wanted to tell you
because you've been brilliant.
It's been dead good being in your class this year
and I quite like writing letters now.

Me and Mandy have promised that when we go to
College
or anywhere like that
we'll write to each other all the time
as well as phoning because you can keep letters.

I'll keep the one I got!
It's from a Secret Admirer.
(I think I know who).

Mum's been in touch with her brother and his wife.
We don't see them much
but they're coming on Christmas Day,
all the family, so that'll be quite nice.

Uncle Warren's dead funny and plays loads
of jokes.
One Christmas he had whoopee cushions
and ugly little wormy things to put in drinks.
Mum wasn't keen on him, then.
But she's changed, I'm amazed
how different she is these days.

I'm really looking forward to it.
My cousin Mel's great
but Clint and Darren are pains.

I hope things are not too bad
for Tracey, too. Poor Trace,
she was always funny but quite sad
but she never whinged like some people.

Me and Mandy think she'll be alright.
She's like that, Tracey.
Mandy thinks she'll come back and see us.

What do you think, Ms?
Do you know where she is?

People are saying she's in care.
I hope it's a nice place and the people are alright.

I'm staying here, with Mum, on Boxing Day.
Mandy's mum said I could go there
but I want to be at home.

            Happy Krimble
                 from
            Kate O. Abidaya

PS I'm glad you're going to your sister's
for Christmas. And thank you
for what you said about adults' problems.

It helped a lot.

About the problems
not being about the children!

It's not my fault!!!

PS 2 I can't wait for my mobile,
Mum says I can choose one tomorrow.
I'll get one with different colours
not just boring old black.
The dead good thing is Mandy's got one
(and my Secret Admirer has!) Fantastico!

PS 3 (sorry!) The first person I'll text is Mandy, next
my Secret Admirer and I'll ask if he'll send me
another letter. I saved his other in a box I made.
(With a satin cover!) Letters Are Ace! Sometimes I
read the ones from Dad. Seeing his writing makes
me feel closer even if it's sad and I hate him. I
save Mandy's notes too. I'll show her when we're
students and we'll have a laugh! Letters are
<u>fantastically</u> cool. (Like Krimble and Mandy
and Secret Admirers!)